HOLE IN THE SNOW

MEYARI MCFARLAND

CONTENTS

Special Offer	v
Other Books by Meyari McFarland:	vii
A Hole in the Snow	1
Author's Note: Artifacts of Awareness	14
1. Sold	15
2: Palace	25
Other Books by Meyari McFarland:	35
Afterword	37
Author Bio	39

SPECIAL OFFER

The rainbow has infinite shades, just as this collection covers the spectrum of fictional possibilities.

From contemporary romances like *The Shores of Twilight Bay* to dark fantasy like *A Lone Red Tree* and out to SF futures in *Child of Spring*, *Iridescent* covers the gamut of time, space and genre.

Meyari McFarland shows her mastery in this first omnibus collection of her short fiction. Twenty-five amazing stories, all with queer characters going on adventures, solving mysteries, and falling in love are here in the first Rainbow Collection.

And now you can get this massive collection of short queer fiction, all of it with the happy endings you love, *for free!*

Sign up here for your free copy of Iridescent now!

OTHER BOOKS BY MEYARI
MCFARLAND:

Day Hunt on the Final Oblivion

Day of Joy

Immortal Sky

A New Path

Following the Trail

Crafting Home

Finding a Way

Go Between

Like Arrows of Fate

Out of Disaster

The Shores of Twilight Bay

Coming Together

Following the Beacon

The Solace of Her Clan

You can find these and many other books at www.MDR-Publishing.com. We are a small independent publisher focusing on LGBT content. Please sign up for our mailing list to get regular updates on the latest preorders and new releases and a free ebook!

Copyright ©2024 by Mary Raichle

Print ISBN: 978-1-64309-125-9

Cover image

Deposit Photo ID# **84089368 by grandfailure**

All rights reserved. No part of this publication may be reproduced or transmitted in any form or by any means, electronic or mechanical, including photocopy, recording or any information storage and retrieval system, without permission in writing from the publisher.

Requests for permission to make copies of any part of the work should be emailed to publisher@mdr-publishing.com.

This book is also available in TPB format from all major retailers.

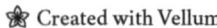 Created with Vellum

This story is dedicated to my mom, gone but never forgotten.

A HOLE IN THE SNOW

*I*gnatz puffed as he hauled one foot through the thigh-deep snow. Ice crystals bloomed in front of him. The cloud enveloped him, crusting his eyelashes and mustache. Around him, the looming pine trees with the heavy branches that drooped like exhausted old men had been transformed into slender spires of glittering white with only the barest hints of green peeking out under the edges of the dense snow.

His knee crunched down into the snow, breaking the inch-thick crust of ice. His boot kicked into the powdery snow underneath. It gave under his weight, like walking up a sand dune that shifted and collapsed underneath you.

Cold or not, Ignatz would take the snow. If all else failed, he could cut the icy crust into blocks, hollow out a cave that would keep him relatively warm. Sand. There was nothing you could do with sand besides bake under the sun, throat closing as you searched for anything to drink. Every single traveler that had ever come through town said that, not that Ignatz had ever gone outside of the valley and the mountains.

This was home, as lonely as it was.

He couldn't leave. Why would he leave? He'd been born here. He would die here someday. Not today. No matter how cold it got, Ignatz wouldn't let the winter snow and wind and chill take him.

Aunt Ruth would be waiting back home. She would be standing next to her little window with its imported glass panes, shawl wrapped round her shoulders as she stared out into the white. That faded old shawl would be the red of congealing blood. It had been crimson when she was young, Ignatz' age. Decades had bled the brightness out, slowly fading it away as the years drained Aunt Ruth's vitality.

She'd gone from a woman the size of the mountains and twice as hard, of the sky overhead and five times as threatening, to an icicle of woman whose words bit as sharply as the frigid air cutting at Ignatz's throat. Not her fault, of course. Her third husband, bitter old Werther Guillory, had to have been the hand that drained Aunt Ruth's life away. He'd died a year ago, leaving Aunt Ruth off in her little cabin built of logs as thick as Ignatz's leg was long. Since old Werther had chased off her cats, she was out there alone, too.

Only Ignatz would live with Aunt Ruth. Even old Werther had spent more time away from the old log house than in it. He had always complained that he wished he had never married Aunt Ruth. She had only ever sniffed and said that he was lucky she put up with his worthless ass given that he wasn't any good for anything.

No one was good enough according to Aunt Ruth.

Not even Ignatz, even though he'd chosen her over his parents, his friends, and the whole world.

Sort of.

He puffed ice crystals as he panted, breaking the ice crust, stomping his foot down, pushing through the snow again and again and again and again.

"Not too far," Ignatz said just to hear something besides the crunch of the ice, the shush of the snow sliding under his boots. "Not too far now. I'll make it home before dark for sure."

Lie. Big one. He had another mile and a half to go before he'd get there. The sun was sliding down the western side of the sky, rolling towards the looming mountains as the day drained away. In a half hour or so, at most, it was going to be dusk. Then dark.

If Ignatz was out once it went dark, he wasn't going to survive the night. Too cold already for that. Which meant that he needed to make himself a hole in the snow, a cave, so that he survived the night. He should have stayed in town.

Why had he insisted that he had to make the trek back out to Aunt Ruth's home when it was already past noon?

Ignatz looked at the pine trees looming around him. The twisting little valley with its frozen river at the center of it was empty of pine. They lurked along the edges of this valley, twenty, thirty yards away from him. The very center of the valley, though, had one tree in a bare five yards away.

The old, old apple tree.

Once, back when Ignatz was a toddler, the tree had stood outside of the old temple. Mother had said that it had bloomed and given everyone in town delicious apples, the best apples in the whole world. Father had laughed and agreed, twirling Mother around as they laughed together.

By the time he was five, the temple had burned down. Mother and Father stopped laughing together. Aunt Ruth had invited them to live in her house beyond the edge of town, out under the heavy looming pines that made midnight under their canopies even at midday.

Aunt Ruth claimed that the old apple tree was cursed. She'd given him the hiding of his life when, as a little boy of just five years, he'd gone and gathered two golden apples that had fallen from its branches. Mother had left by that point, promising Ignatz's help to Aunt Ruth and apologizing to him privately that she just couldn't stand to live with Aunt Ruth one minute longer.

The bruises on her face and back and wrists had inspired Ignatz to smile and promise that of course he would stay with Aunt Ruth. He'd be fine. Mother had cried as she left him behind with Aunt Ruth's hand on his shoulder.

Most of the town had moved to the far side of the valley. Further from Aunt Ruth. Further from the apple tree.

"You bring curses into my home?" Aunt Ruth had bellowed as she walloped Ignatz despite his cries and pleading. "After all I do for you, you bring curses into my home!"

She'd taken the apples and thrown them into the midden heap, stomping around and complaining about Ignatz's evil and how he was going to grow up to be worse than his no-good grandfather. As bad as his mother who'd abandoned Aunt Ruth when she turned twenty, going into town to live and be happy well away from Aunt Ruth.

Their whole family had slowly filtered away. His mother had moved to the ocean, weeks travel away. His father had shrugged, eyes distant and sad, and taken a new wife, going to live with her family further north, over the pass that snowed shut each year. Aunt Ruth had no children. She drove away every husband she managed to find, even old Werther though he hung on the longest of them all.

She was alone, other than Ignatz who had never forgotten his promise to his mother.

He'd spent his life by her side, watching as people moved farther and farther and farther away. Twenty years ago, the town had been an hour's walk away. A landslide had destroyed the fields, killed forty people, and the town moved three hours walk away. Ten years ago, they'd moved even further after the well went dry. A trip into the town full of strangers now took two full days, minimum. Sometimes three.

Aunt Ruth refused to leave her home in the looming pine woods.

"I was born here, and I'll die here," Aunt Ruth always said, glaring at Ignatz with narrowed eyes that dared him to go somewhere else without her permission.

"It is home," was all Ignatz ever said in reply because that was true.

Even if it was a cold home with a cold old woman who hadn't had a kind word to say since before Ignatz's mother was born.

Ignatz smiled. Winced. Took a deep breath and stomped his way through the snow towards the old apple tree. He wouldn't tell Aunt Ruth he spent the night here. Better that way. She couldn't beat him anymore, her bones had gone as fragile as freshly formed ice overtop the river, but her tongue had only gotten sharper over the years.

The snow level dropped to knee-deep. Then calf. Then, as Ignatz's panted breath went from clouds of ice crystals to fog to nothing at all, to a bare inch of rapidly melting snow.

Green grass ringed the apple tree.

There were tiny white flowers in the grass. Sweet clover. Ignatz stood at the edge of the circle of green that he hadn't seen from a distance. It only revealed itself once he made the decision to shelter here.

The apple tree rose over his head like the arches of the new temple they'd built in town, only grander. Wilder. Much more beautiful against the gold and red and growing purple of the dusk sky. Grey-green lichen covered its twisted branches like a rough-coated sheep who'd gone wild. Standing in the inch-deep snow, Ignatz couldn't smell anything. Snow. Cold, distant. His own sweat and the sourness of his mouth as he panted and shivered and remembered those beautiful gold apples from so long ago.

Thirty years had gone by.

He could still remember the weight and heft of the first apple in his little hands. That day, with the sun beating down on his head and the sweet smell of clover under his bare feet, the apples had felt like metal, not fruit. They'd been smooth and shiny, yet when he had lifted one to his nose, it filled his head with the heady joy of the sweet crispy apples that Mother used to make cobbler.

Ignatz had licked his lips, looked around to see if Aunt Ruth or her husband old Werther was watching. If anyone was there. No one was. Not a single person came to the edge of the fields or looked out their doors towards him.

He'd eaten that first apple. Sugar-sweet on his tongue, every bite had filled him with joy, with energy, with a sort of settled happiness that he'd thought only happened in stories. That was why he'd picked up two other fallen apples. That was why he'd brought them home. Aunt Ruth and old Werther needed that sort of joy. They had so little happiness, so few smiles, that Ignatz had known that the golden apples would make things better.

For him as well as for them.

The midden heap had caught fire in the middle of the night. It had burned so fiercely that the ground was glassy in the morning. Nothing was left other than a blackened, ashy pit.

Ignatz shivered.

"They rejected the gift," Ignatz whispered. "That's why. Is that why everyone left? Is that why the well went dry?"

He didn't want to believe it, but the priestess in town always claimed that the gods weren't happy with them. That was why so many bad things happened, why so many children died before they reached adulthood.

No one had expected Ignatz to live, not living with bitter old Aunt Ruth who drove off everyone who'd ever loved her.

Ignatz stared at his hands. They were bigger than they had been at five, obviously. The apples he'd carried home with such difficulty would be easy to carry now, two to a palm instead of carrying them in his arms because they were so large. Under his gloves, his hands were unmarred by the many little injuries of chopping wood, hunting, fishing, toiling for Aunt Ruth.

He'd never broken a bone. He'd never gotten sick. His hair had been dark as a child but now it was as golden as that first apple so long ago. His eyes had a hint of gold in their brown, making them glimmer in the light of the fire.

Aunt Ruth always snarled at him when she saw it.

"I changed," Ignatz whispered as he took that step from snow to snow-white clover filled grass. "After I ate that apple, I changed."

Aunt Ruth hadn't.

Years, decades, had gone by, and Aunt Ruth was the same vicious woman she'd been when he brought the golden apples to her in a vain attempt to bring her joy. Every single person she'd ever interacted with, family or otherwise, had left.

Except Ignatz who couldn't be destroyed no matter how cruel Aunt Ruth got.

Who wouldn't give up on her, no matter how pointless his quest was.

The apple tree bloomed as he approached. Its mossy branches shed their lichen fur. Delicate white flowers unfurled like dancers spinning midsummer prayers in the town square. Ignatz licked his lip and reached up to caress one petal.

The petal shimmered golden at the edges as leaves burst forth all over the old apple tree. Gold spread over the rest of the blossom, then across the leaves bracketing it. Ignatz watched, heart pounding in his chest.

This was what had happened when he was five. Exactly what had happened, actually. The snow was different. He'd come in the spring, not in the depths of winter. The old apple tree had gleamed as he ran from his mother's house out to Aunt Ruth's as he'd promised to do every day once Mother left Aunt Ruth's home.

He hadn't wanted to. Ignatz had forgotten just how vicious Aunt Ruth was over the years. He'd ignored her harsh words, the beatings, the dark glares. It was easier to focus on everyone else leaving than on Aunt Ruth who punished him for ever raising his eyes towards her glittering black eyes filled with hate.

That day, thirty years ago, Ignatz had gladly detoured away from the path to explore whatever gleamed in the old apple tree. He'd wished so hard that it would be something that could fix his family, that could make Aunt Ruth stop driving everyone away the way a sheepherder drove his flock.

The apples should have been the answer to his prayer.

"You tried to save me," Ignatz whispered as he rested his hand on the branch. "Your magic, you poured it into those apples and I... I was a fool."

A breeze ruffled the luxurious leaves covering the old apple tree. They sighed as if he'd missed the point yet again. Ignatz frowned and cocked his head to the side.

"My life would be so much easier if everyone just said what they meant outright," Ignatz huffed. He shook his head as the golden blossom shivered like it was going to transform into another apple. "No, that's not a request, love. That's just me being frustrated with myself. I was a fool, you know. A very young fool who thought that there was a way to save

Aunt Ruth from herself. I should've realized when the midden heap burned."

The tree's leaves rustled again. This time it felt like a rueful laugh, a fond smile, a pat on the shoulder from someone he'd known for a very long time. Which he had. The tree and he went back a long time.

"I miss everyone," Ignatz whispered as he leaned his forehead against the branch. "Mother, Father, my friends, the townsfolk. I miss them all. But I can't leave. This... This is home. Here, this valley, these mountains. They're home.

His breath caught in his chest, lungs aching, as the apple tree reached higher and higher into the sky, capturing the colors of gold from the setting sun, purple from the clouds, scarlet from the drop of blood at the corner of his mouth where he'd bitten through his lip.

For one endless, aching moment, he felt his body as he'd been thirty years ago. Small, bright, curious, hopeful; the Ignatz of five years old mingled with the thirty-five-year-old Ignatz.

You can go back, the apple tree seemed to say. You can try again. Just ask.

Ignatz shuddered. Swallowed down the sour-acid at the back of his throat even though his entire mouth had gone dry as bone.

"Oh, love, no," Ignatz whispered. "No, not that."

He stepped closer so that he could rest his forehead against the trunk of the apple tree. There was a pulse under his fingers, against his cheek, slow and deep and full of joy. The same joy he'd felt all those years ago.

"It's you I can't leave," Ignatz whispered as he felt his heartbeat slow into time with the pulse of the apple tree. "Not Aunt Ruth. That's why I've stayed. This feeling. Not taking care of her. When I leave the valley, when I get to far from you, I lose the joy that comes from you."

Something like a start of surprise jerked the apple tree. Ignatz smiled and stepped back enough that he could look up towards the stars slowly twinkling into life overhead. Royal purple studded with rare diamonds went velvet black with grand swathes of glittering stars. A broad river of stars swooped across the sky, beautiful and perfect.

Just like the apple tree.

Ignatz smiled. "I know what I want. I want to take you with me, love. I want to move to the new town, make a life there. Away from Aunt Ruth and her nastiness. I just don't know how to do that without harming you and killing Aunt Ruth."

The apple blossoms, all golden now, dropped their petals and grew in seconds into apples that gleamed like metal in the distant, cold light of the stars. Ignatz blinked and started as the apples fell around him.

Every single one.

They dropped one after another until he was surrounded by a harvest of unbearably beautiful golden apples in a ring around the old apple tree. He opened his mouth to ask, then jerked back a step, cracking his shoulder against the tree trunk, as the apples began to steam and rot and split open.

They fogged up into the night. As Ignatz watched, the tendrils of steam turned into a true fog that curled around both Ignatz and the apple tree. It was so thick that the sky disappeared. He couldn't see the clover under his feet. There was nothing but the fog and the apple tree strong and sturdy behind his shoulder.

It felt like minutes when the fog faded. Or maybe hours. Days?

Ignatz couldn't tell until the fog blew away entirely. His jaw dropped as he stared out at the valley. The snow was gone. Off in the east, the sun rose over the mountains, sending shafts of gold down to land directly on Ignatz and the apple tree. He raised one hand to protect his eyes.

"Ho!"

Ignatz nearly fell down in his shock. Four people, three women, one man, stood off by the line of looming pine trees at the edge of the valley. They stared at Ignatz with something like awe, something like fear in their eyes. One man stood with them; his hand clenched on an axe.

"Where'd you come from?" the man called.

"I'd ask you that," Ignatz replied. "This... It's spring. This is spring, yes?"

The four of them stared at each other before turning to stare even more curiously at Ignatz.

"Yes," the man said. "Would think that was obvious."

"No," Ignatz said. He put one hand on the trunk of the apple tree, his blessed apple tree. "No, it's not. It was midwinter. I was on my way out to Aunt Ruth's place. She... How can it be spring?"

The man started. "Ignatz? Are you Ignatz Lauwers?"

Ignatz nodded.

"I'll be," the man said, rubbing the back of his head. "You disappeared five years ago. Old lady Ruth died over the winter. No one knew until months after the fact. She refused to leave her house, refused to let anyone stay with her. Said you'd be back because you were cursed."

"Not me," Ignatz said, shaking his head and sighing that Aunt Ruth got her wish, twisted as it was. She'd died in her home as she'd always wanted. "Blessed. Aunt Ruth was cursed. It was why everyone left, why I stayed. I could handle it. No one else could."

The women frowned at him when he claimed to be blessed. Justified, but what else could he call it? His apple tree had given him so much, including his freedom. Perhaps he could finally give it what it wanted: people to live around it, to share its joy.

"That's blasphemy," the man said with slow, ponderous seriousness that didn't reach his eyes.

Ignatz smiled and stepped away from the tree. Every step he took towards the four of them made delicate white sweet clover bloom in the grass. Birds swooped in from the forest to flit around his head. The smell of apples, impossible golden apples, hung in the air around him.

He watched their eyes go wide as he approached. When Ignatz held out his hand for the man to shake, his skin gleamed the metallic gold of the apple he'd eaten all those years ago. He expected the man to step back, to refuse to take his hand.

He didn't.

"Ignatz Lauwers," Ignatz said as a crooked smile curled his lips.

"Dimitri Legrand," the man, Dimitri, replied, eyes wide.

"I'm honored," Ignatz said.

"These are my sisters," Dimitri said when the oldest tugged at his elbow. "Charlotte, Alexia and Sarina. We were harvesting when we saw you."

"Blessed," Charlotte asked without asking.

Ignatz nodded. "Yes. I believe so. It's a long story. I could help you harvest? Tell you while we work. I, ah, suppose I have nowhere else to be now that Aunt Ruth is gone. Strange to think that. She seemed eternal."

Dimitri nodded slowly, once, twice, and then again harder. "Please. A story always makes the work go faster. How's it start?"

Ignatz laughed as the joy filled his heart in a flood. "There used to be a temple right over there, by the apple tree. Those apples fed the pilgrims who came to visit year-round. It bore so many apples that the branches had to be supported, all of them perfect and sweet and delicious. The apples never went bad, no matter how far into the year you went. It was said that you could get a wish if you showed up when the apples turned to gold. But then, not more than a few days after my Aunt Ruth moved to town when her second husband left her, the temple burned down."

He moved off into the forest with Dimitri, Charlotte, Alexia, and Sarina. A new start. A new life. Ignatz smiled and let his joy carry him along as he forged a path free from Aunt Ruth at last.

AUTHOR'S NOTE: ARTIFACTS OF AWARENESS

A lot of my characters are unreasonably stubborn. I might, possibly, be rather stubborn myself so I'm never surprised when it comes out in my stories. Write what you know, right?

Still, Kennet in Artifacts of Awareness, takes stubborn to whole new heights. He's one of those characters who gets kicked and then snarls as he gets back up over and over and over again. I think that Kennet's blind determination to keep on going no matter what happens to him would make total sense to Ignatz which is why I decided to share a sample of Kennet's story.

Hope you enjoy the sample!

1. SOLD

Heat sweltered in the dimness of the tent, intensified by the dozen or so naked bodies pressed entirely too close. Kennet ignored the heat. Ignored the two slaves on either side of them with their sun-browned skin slowly sweating rivers down their sides; his sweat couldn't cool him when they were all pressed so close together.

Outside he heard the rapid patter of the slave merchant as he talked up the current slave on the block. Midday was a terrible time for selling slaves but the lot was so large that the sale had been going on since the predawn dew evaporated away.

Two years. Two years, nine masters and three continents later Kennet knew better than to fight being sold, no matter how much he resented the loss of his freedom.

Kennet refused to growl as he knelt in the slave's tent for his turn on the auction block. Why waste the energy? He wouldn't accomplish anything other than a beating and probably would end up being sold to a worse, more abusive, master. No one but a fool fought on the auction block. Well, a fool and Kennet.

The first time he'd been sold he'd fought so hard that it had taken hours for him to wake up from the damage the Alliance guards had inflicted. Finding himself in chains with a slave collar had resulted in an explosion of violence that had sent him to Inina's sheltering arms for another long period of unconsciousness and an even longer recuperation.

Every sale since then had resulted in less violence, if no less resentment. Alliance slave training designed to destroy his sense of self and ability to act independently hadn't been enough to grind down Kennet's desire for freedom. It had only made him hide his anger and use it as fuel for his will to resist.

Of course, if Juraj hadn't been obviously destined to be Elder Danek's favorite blood slave pet Kennet might still be free.

Not that it was Juraj's fault, really. Kennet had to admit that Juraj had done everything in his power to stay out of Danek's sight. He licked his lip free of sweat, tasting the thin broth they'd been given last night along with the dirt he'd slept on. No, Juraj wasn't to blame, not with his gentle words and hesitant touches that had always made Kennet want to protect him against the world.

Crumbling Hells, the kid used to damn near disappear inside himself whenever Danek's power moved through the people around them. They'd see the people around them stiffen and stop in place like puppets whose strings had been tangled. When Kennet had turned Juraj's face was as blank as everyone else's. Kennet still had no idea how Juraj had made himself appear like one of Danek's pawns who populated their home town. Had to be magic of some sort but it didn't match the magic that he'd seen proper mages do since leaving home.

"You wouldn't be able to do it," Juraj had laughed one night as they hid together in the barn after a round of breathless, silent sex under the rafters. *"You're smart, Kennet, but you've got as much magic in you as a rock. In Inina's name, the rocks around here have more magic than you do!"*

"Rude," Kennet had laughed before sucking a mark on Juraj's chest that made him fight back a moan. *"Not my fault you live in the ruins of an ancient building."*

"Still true," Juraj had chuckled as the barn cats meowed and hissed around them, hunting mice in the hay surrounding them. *"The only way you could feel Elder Danek's power was if your soul was ripped out and replaced by someone else's."*

That was a joke, Kennet thought as the slave in front of him was brought out for his round at auction. Juraj's soul probably had been ripped out of him only to be replaced by Elder Danek's mind and soul. He shifted his legs again, glaring at the ground between his knees so that he wouldn't glare at the guards quietly complaining about the heat or the auctioneer and his constant jabber outside the tent.

Kennet hadn't left home. He'd run away in a panic, just barely ahead of Danek's damned blood slaves and the Empire's Guards. It was his own damned fault, frankly. Spring Festival had come around again and he'd seen the way Danek was eyeing Juraj. Fourteen, lean and pretty with shining brown hair and those perfect brown eyes; Juraj had been enough to tempt a saint, not that either Kennet or Danek were saints.

All it had taken was Juraj skittering away from Danek's hand with that covertly panicked expression for Kennet to slam a fist into Danek's face before grabbing Juraj and running for the hills. It was a minor thing anywhere else in the world but Danek had taken it insanely seriously. Kennet had hidden in the forest around Spider Mountain, dodging giant spiders and acidic borjaz, until Juraj had found him somehow.

"You've been declared an exile," Juraj had panted, face pale and clammy, spider webs caught on his hair and shirt. Terror all but radiated off him. *"They're already hunting for you."*

"Fuck," was all Kennet had said before kissing Juraj one last time and running for the border. Kennet knew perfectly well that Danek had wanted him dead, not exiled. No one who challenged Danek survived. Most of them ended up sacrificed at the secret rites that Kennet had carefully kept from Juraj or torn apart in various creative ways. Frankly, Juraj's gasped words of warning were probably the only reason he was still alive.

Kennet still wasn't sure if he should ask Inina to bless Juraj for that or Haraldr to strike him down for sending Kennet into a fate worse than death.

He shook off the past. Kennet dismissed his frequent daydreams of getting his freedom and going off somewhere to raise rabbits. That wasn't going to happen so he paid attention to his environment as the last slave in front of him was pulled up onto the block. The auctioneer was one of the ones who tried to pump the crowd up with chatter about the slave on the block.

Kennet raised an eyebrow when the auctioneer described the boy trembling on the block as 'untouched' and 'obedient'. The kid was young, sure, but it was obvious from where Kennet knelt that he was anything but untouched and the scars on his back spoke of someone who'd been punished many times in his short lifetime.

Once the bidding started it didn't make much difference. Rich people, presumably they were rich given the prices being offered on other slaves before, bid on the boy. The price started low and didn't go much higher despite the auctioneer's efforts to entice more bids. Kennet wiggled his toes to get circulation back to his feet as money changed hands and the boy was led away. He smiled grimly at the way the boy jerked against his new master's leash. Not bright but he could have predicted it from the marks on the boy's back. When the auctioneer came back for Kennet he stood, waiting with a calm exterior that didn't match the frustrated rage inside.

"Skills, skills, what skills does this one have?" the auctioneer muttered. He didn't bother to look in Kennet's eyes, instead scanning a little card that his former master had filled out.

"Fighting, cooking, farming, fucking and I can read Old Vorenic," Kennet said because who knew what the hell the auctioneer would come up with. His former master sure as hell wouldn't have given an accurate account of his abilities. He'd sold Kennet to get money to cover his gambling debts.

"Huh, reading, that's unusual," the auctioneer said. This time he actually looked Kennet over as he nodded at the scars covering Kennet's body. "Might even believe the fighting. You've got the build for it. Right, come along."

He led Kennet out onto the auction block, already putting on his strut and bluster. Outside the tent the sun was a hell of a lot hotter than it'd been inside but at least there was a breeze to help the sweat chill his skin. Kennet still wasn't used to the heat this far south. The sun seemed twice the size it was back home and at least three times as hot. His paler skin stuck out amidst the dark elm-brown colors of everyone else's faces.

The crowd of rich bidders looking up at the auction block was pretty standard. Most looked like they were ready to be anywhere else, eyes shielded by a hand held up against the sun's rays. Quite a few were dressed in the rough canvas and leather that military types used in Penhale though most of them were talking off to one side instead of looking at Kennet.

Way in the back there was what looked like a noble in fine silk clothes. He was surrounded by guards who looked like they'd kill anyone who got too close. Given the assassination attempts that Kennet had heard about against the king's family, he could understand any noble being nervous about going out in public right now. It wasn't very likely that Kennet would be chosen by nobles. He had no skills that a noble would need, outside of breeding stock.

"This one is the prize of the lot," the auctioneer said as proudly as if he hadn't said it nine times already today and that was just when Kennet had been listening. "Strong, well trained in fighting and very obedient, this one. Not only that but he's intelligent as well. He's learned to read Old Vorenic and cook. If that's not to your taste, he's from good farming stock and can work on your farm with no complaints or training. What am I bid?"

Kennet helped the pitch a little bit by discretely tensing his arms and legs to emphasize the muscles there. He made sure to keep his face calm and as close to Juraj's blank nothingness as Kennet had ever been able to get. The bidding started four times as high as the previous slave and went up dramatically when the auctioneer had Kennet turn around slowly so that he could describe what good breeding stock Kennet was. A couple of quick hip thrusts as he turned around made the bidding go much faster. By the time the price was up to twenty-three gold Kennet was wryly amused because the auctioneer kept adding to Kennet's 'skills' every time the bidding went up.

"One hundred fifty gold."

Silence echoed across the auction block. The bid came from the back of the crowd from the older noble surrounded by guards. Kennet stared at him along with half the crowd, unsure what to make of the bid. It was more than what he'd been sold for totaling all his sales up over his last nine masters. Even his guards turned to stare at the old noble though they only did it for a moment. It took a moment for the auctioneer to splutter to a stop as he finally realized that the bid was real. As soon as he did, he lit up with delight.

"One hundred fifty gold is offered!" the auctioneer exclaimed. "Do I have one fifty-five? Anyone? Anyone?"

Only shuffling feet and awkward coughs answered him. Kennet shut his mouth and blanked his face again. A price that high wasn't going to get any counter offers, especially with a crowd that had already bought a small army of slaves. The auctioneer clapped his hands once while grinning at the size of his commission.

"Sold!"

Kennet moved off the block without being tugged, going off to the side where one of the noble's guards came forward with a little bag full of money. He didn't resist as a leash was attached to his collar. There wasn't much point to resisting. After spending that much money on Kennet, he'd probably be kept on a very short leash until his new master was sure that Kennet wasn't going to try to run.

Honestly, after this long, Kennet knew he was always going to be a slave, no matter how much that made the anger burn and snarl inside of him. At least as a slave he had someone to protect him. Danek wasn't likely to take on a master just to get at him. He might try and buy Kennet specifically so that he could be killed or, worse, have his mind ripped out by becoming a blood slave, but being a slave might (might) be safer than being free.

The old noble looked Kennet over with eyes that seemed just as threatening as Elder Danek's but without that shimmer of power that always made Kennet's hair stand on end and his common sense run away. After a studying him for long enough that the auctioneer came out with the next slave on the block, the noble nodded once as he turned to lead Kennet and his guards away from the slave market.

His guards surrounded them, one keeping a tight grip on Kennet's arm despite his lack of resistance. Away from the slave market it seemed even hotter. The buildings bracketing the streets seemed to reflect the heat of the sun down on Kennet's naked body. It didn't appear to bother the old noble or his guards but they'd been born to this sort of thing. Kennet hoped idly, and then dismissed the thought as ridiculous, that somewhere he might get something to drink.

Eight blocks later, they ended up in a closed carriage that sweltered even worse than the tent under the afternoon sun. Kennet wheezed at the heat filling the carriage as he climbed in. The noble raised one eyebrow as he didn't seem to be affected by the heat at all. He settled in on his cushions with a contented little wiggle of his shoulders, gesturing for Kennet to sit on the opposite bench along with his guards.

Asking questions of someone that stern didn't seem like a good idea, not when bracketed on either side by burly guards who were as big as Kennet or a little bigger. Their grips on Kennet's wrists were tight enough that he could feel the bones shift. Kennet deliberately kept his arms as loose as possible to encourage the belief that he actually was obedient.

The old man didn't seem like most of the nobles Kennet had encountered since his exile. Sure, he was dressed in rich silks with very discreet and somber embroidery but he didn't say anything harsh or smack Kennet around. There were no snide comments about Kennet's very distinct stench or preemptive displays of authority. To his relief, the noble also didn't decide that Kennet should immediately suck his cock.

"I find myself relieved," the old man said after a few minutes of sweltering but relatively peaceful quiet as the carriage jolted along the rutted streets. "You are far more quiet and circumspect than I expected."

Kennet didn't think that a response was required but one of the guards elbowed him so he shifted a little and bowed at the waist towards the old man, doing his best not to move his arms. "Thank you, Master."

"Oh, I am not your Master, young man," the old man said with a little sniff accompanied by a wrinkled nose of distaste. "You will meet him soon enough. I must caution you to be on your best behavior when we arrive. Despite the sum spent to acquire you, any inappropriate actions on your part will result in your immediate termination."

That was a clear enough 'don't fuck this up' that Kennet bowed a little more deeply and nodded. "Yes, Sir. I understand, Sir."

"Excellent."

The old man turned to look out the one partially open window of the carriage as if the other occupants no longer existed. Kennet sat back against the cushions between his two keepers to wait for their journey to end. Asking questions really didn't seem like a good idea. Of course, asking questions rarely was a good idea for a slave no matter who had bought him.

It took a bit over an hour for the carriage to wind its way through the streets. They went from rutted dirt roads that jerked them side to side onto cobblestones that tried to rattle the teeth out of Kennet's head. At one point they crossed a bridge that was surprisingly smooth. The water in the air was a brief blessing of coolness that was immediately swallowed by heat on the other side. Thankfully, the road on that side was much smoother, as if they'd used stone blocks instead of cobbles for paving the road.

He'd heard one of Pensri's Temple bells ring shortly after they started out. A second one rang just as they rolled to a gentle stop wherever they'd been going. Kennet let the old man go first, following second when the guards not too gently nudged him towards the door. It seemed like a bad idea to tread on the old man's heels but pissing off the guards would be stupid at this point. If he was lucky he might have gotten a good master, for once.

"Whoa," Kennet breathed once he slipped out of the carriage and stood next to the old man.

The bulk of the Penhale Royal Palace loomed over him, white marble carved in extravagant depictions of flowers and trees. Kennet's empty stomach sank as he remembered the quiet murmurs of assassination attempts and betrayals at the highest levels.

No, this wasn't better, Kennet thought. He might have just stepped out of the frying pan and into the fire.

2: PALACE

"*Blessed Inina, save my sorry ass from whatever I've gotten into this time,*" Kennet thought as the bulk of the royal palace towered over him. The damn thing was so huge and imposing that it drove the air out of his already empty lungs.

It was huge, easily six stories high with turrets equally spaced across the length of it and wings extending out behind towards gardens that looked large enough to swallow the entire village that Kennet had grown up in. Several outbuildings that looked the size of small mountains surrounded it, along with a huge wall that looked wide enough to hold his family's home on top of its upper edge.

People bustled around, all clothed, all clean, all obviously free. Kennet's balls shriveled as he tried to swallow around the lump of fear in his throat. What the hell was he doing here? He wasn't good enough of a slave for this place! Hell, he wasn't good enough of a man for it! All Kennet had ever been was a short-tempered farmer who'd gotten in over his head.

"Come along, now," the old noble snapped when Kennet didn't immediately follow him into the palace.

The guards shoved Kennet towards the front door, making sure that he kept moving even when his feet stumbled to a stop at the top of the stairs. A slave still dirty from the dealers really shouldn't walk on a cream carpet like that. Or the ivory marble floor that followed; it was a joy of coolness for his bare feet but he left footprints behind that made him cringe. The perfectly pristine stairs that followed didn't have a speck of dust on them until Kennet walked up them, dropping sweat, bits of dirt and mortified embarrassment as he went.

Kennet did his best to keep silent despite the urge to curse at everyone and everything. This was absolutely impossible. Things like this didn't happen. He wanted to shout it to the vaulted ceilings with their exquisite murals before running right back out that massive front door to cower by the oven-like carriage. Slaves like him did not get bought for impossible prices and brought to palaces like this. It just didn't happen.

He recognized the gibbering fear as the ever-present remnants of his Alliance slave training. His trainer had done is best to beat down Kennet's sense of identity until it died but he'd never totally succeeded. Kennet had learned how to fake being broken before his trainer had figured out that he wasn't being fully successful with the torture, rape and personality altering spells.

All of the fear making your heart pound is external, Kennet told himself. *You're safe. They wanted you in particular. The old man was looking for someone just like you. Doesn't fucking matter that you're filthy and you stink. They want a filthy stinking slave for some damned reason. You belong here, you're wanted, this is who you're supposed to be so stop acting like a fucking moron!*

That his mental voice sounded like his Alliance slave trainer made Kennet want to throw up but the harsh mental talk let him square his shoulders and stop shaking as he walked. If the royal fucking family wanted a filthy slave fresh from the auction block then they wanted a slave fresh from the auction block. Kennet only hoped that he could keep them from finding out about his Alliance training. King Barabbas had declared such training illegal and all Alliance-trained slaves were to be put down as soon as they were found.

Given that every other Alliance-trained slave he'd ever seen was a nonentity who lacked the will to even piss without orders Kennet couldn't blame him but it just meant that he had to be careful about how he reacted to being in the palace.

"Your Majesty," the old man said over Kennet's strangled noise of shock, "I have returned with a promising slave. I believe he may meet your requirements."

"Thank you, Alexio," King Barabbas said. "Bring him in, please."

The room wasn't a throne room. In fact it was a small, relatively dark office with bookshelves along one wall and deep green curtains over the one, extremely narrow, window. There was a huge desk that looked big enough for three or four people to sleep on if they got cozy, not that anyone would do anything like that on a desk that ornate and imposing. The room smelled like lemon oil and melon, the green sort that he used to pick on his fifth master's farm.

King Barabbas himself sat behind the desk, reclining in a chair that looked to be equally ornate, though Kennet could see some good padding on the seat and back.

King Barabbas looked mildly amused by Kennet's wide eyes and stunned expression. That was good because Kennet didn't think he could manage anything other response, except maybe kneeling and pressing his dirty, sweating forehead to the cream and green carpet on the floor. What the hell did a king need with a slave like Kennet?

His guards didn't let Kennet kneel. Each of them caught one elbow to prevent Kennet's nearly automatic response to being in the presence of quality. It wasn't just the Alliance training that screamed at him to kneel. All his life he'd known to bow and scrape when faced with people of power. Danek had always smiled like a wolf seeing a fawn when Kennet swallowed, bowed and then scurried away.

To Kennet's horror, both of the princes were standing behind King Barabbas. The older prince Didymos was darker than his younger brother Telamon, though both of them were significantly darker than Kennet would ever be. Surprisingly, Didymos stared at Kennet with a friendly smile on his face. Telamon just eyed Kennet calmly and then nodded once as if he passed muster. King Barabbas gestured for the guards to leave them, which finally allowed Kennet to go down on one knee. Given the situation he really didn't think he should be standing but none of them looked as though they expected a full protestation out of him.

"You can fight?" King Barabbas asked Kennet.

The direct address made him start before he caught himself and nodded. "Yes, your Majesty. I'm trained as a bodyguard and I've fought a fair bit for my masters. Mostly pit fighting, not real fighting."

"I would think that pit fighting was real fighting," King Barabbas observed as if Kennet had just said something incredibly interesting.

"Ah, not really, your Majesty," Kennet said while cursing his too-eager tongue. "It's a bit showy compared to proper battlefield combat. Never been part of a proper war, only bodyguard work a couple of times and the pits."

"Point taken," King Barabbas said, nodding that he understood. "But you're familiar with fighting in close quarters against desperate odds."

"Yes, your Majesty," Kennet said a great deal more slowly than before.

The way King Barabbas phrased it made him very worried about what he'd been bought to do. King Barabbas stroked the tip of his thumb over his bottom lip while studying Kennet carefully. Kennet didn't swing his hand so that it covered his genitals. No point to it when they'd already gotten an eyeful, but he wished that he could. The considering expression on King Barabbas' face made his cock and balls shrivel even further than they had before.

It wasn't difficult to link the many assassination attempts that had plagued the royal family of Penhale with Kennet's presence there, especially given that Prince Didymos looked at him with enough interest and bright enthusiasm that his assignment seemed perfectly clear.

Bodyguard to one of the princes wasn't exactly what he'd expected when he'd been brought to the slave market but then, he'd expected to be sold to a pit manager or another large farm holder. This was honestly more likely to get him killed than either of those jobs. Kennet didn't think he had any chance of surviving the intrigues of the palace but then you never knew.

After all, Kennet hadn't expected to escape Elder Danek and he'd done that. Sure he'd gone from bad to worse when the Alliance declared him an unwanted refugee suitable for slavery but he'd survived them. He'd gone through training, nine separate master and entirely too long as a pit fighter, though he certainly had the scars to show for that.

Sometimes Kennet thought that the Gods laughed at you as you struggled to deal with the shitholes they flung you into. This had to be the nicest shithole yet, even with Kennet's stench stinking the place up.

"Good," King Barabbas said while studying Kennet as if he was seeing straight into Kennet's soul. "You will be my heir's bodyguard. There are other guards who will always be around, but that is not your concern. Your sole duty is to stay by his side at all times. You eat with him, sleep with him, bathe with him, go everywhere with him. No one is authorized to separate the two of you. If anyone tries, you are authorized to execute them on the spot, no matter what their rank or position is."

"Er, and if he takes a lover?" Kennet asked. What the hell, how was the kid going to get an heir with someone watching all the damned time?

"You will watch over them both and make sure that the lover doesn't attack him," King Barabbas answered in such a stern tone that Kennet immediately bowed his head in assent.

The humiliated whine that came from the princes' corner of the room made Kennet fight against a smirk. Apparently Prince Didymos didn't like the idea of someone watching him fuck any more than Kennet liked the idea of doing it. Granted, Kennet understood King Barabbas' reasoning but it would still be as embarrassing as all fuck to deal with if it came to that.

A little puddle of sweat formed under his bent knee as the comment about lovers attacking sank into Kennet's mind. He hadn't thought that the betrayals had gotten that bad but King Barabbas looked so serious when Kennet glanced up at him that he realized that Kennet would literally have to watch everyone and everything. There were no friends, no allies, no trusted lovers, not if he wanted to keep Prince Didymos alive.

"Father," Prince Didymos protested weakly enough that Kennet knew that he'd already realized there was no getting around King Barabbas' orders. "Is this really necessary?"

"I will not lose you," King Barabbas murmured in a much more tender and loving tone of voice that made Kennet wish he'd mastered the art of being functionally invisible around his betters. Even with his training he'd never managed it.

"I will not lose either of you. Telamon's not the primary focus of the attacks so far but he will have a slave body guard as well. You must do this, Didymos. Neither your mother nor I could deal with losing you."

Prince Didymos sighed. "Yes, Father. Shall I take him to get cleaned up and to get a proper uniform?"

"Yes," King Barabbas replied.

Kennet raised his head only to drop it again at the fierce look in King Barabbas' eyes. He stayed there for a long moment, hopefully long enough to convey his respect towards King Barabbas. It was always tricky figuring out how much respect to show when he met new people. Some expected outrageous levels of respect while others saw even minimal levels as insulting from a slave who must never have been properly broken. He must have judged the time well enough because the fierce look in King Barabbas' eyes had faded to something rather less threatening by the time Kennet raised his head.

"Go," King Barabbas ordered, the unspoken expectation that Kennet lived only as long as Prince Didymos did hanging in the air between them. "Keep him alive. That's all you have to do."

"Yes, your Majesty," Kennet said with another quick bow of his head. "I'll do my best at that."

Prince Didymos gestured for Kennet to follow him, only to start in surprise when Kennet insisted on checking outside the door before letting him go first. While Prince Didymos looked irritated by the precaution, Kennet could see an approving look on King Barabbas' face so he didn't let that bother him.

Other guards surrounded the two of them as they headed up the hallway into the Palace's private quarters. Six seemed like a good number but Kennet found himself wondering who they reported to and whether he could demand to check their weapons for poison. Maybe he was overreacting but the whole country was full of stories of assassination attempts. Over the last year he'd heard more and more stories about people attacking Penhale's royal family in increasingly creative ways. If even a fraction of those stories were true then Kennet had his work cut out for him.

He'd have to check Prince Didymos' food, his water, verify that his sheets were properly washed and the towels hadn't been dosed with something. There would have to be checks of the people he interacted with on a daily basis, from the servants up to his friends. Anyone could be bought off for a sufficient price and those that couldn't be bought might be spelled to do things they normally wouldn't.

"This shouldn't be too bad," Prince Didymos said cheerfully as they entered what had to be his quarters. His face went red when Kennet caught his arm, keeping him from entering the suite before the guards and then Kennet could check it. "Then again, maybe it will be worse than I expect."

"It's going to be invasive, humiliating, horrifying and probably the most embarrassing thing you've ever experienced, your Highness," Kennet replied once he'd pulled the apparently slightly younger man into the suite with him. "Sorry, but I only live as long as you do so I'm going to take this deadly seriously."

"You could at least tell me your name," Prince Didymos complained while glaring at him. The other guards looked as though they were trying to hide their surprise at how seriously he was taking his new assignment.

Kennet stared at him, surprised that a prince would even care about a slave's name. "Kennet. My name is Kennet, Prince Didymos."

"Kennet," Prince Didymos repeated, though on his tongue

the hard final 't' turned into something that was almost a 'sh' sound. "Pleased to meet you, Kennet."

"Pleased to meet you too, Highness," Kennet replied with a little snort of amusement. "Now let me check this place out properly so I can tell where the threats against you might come from."

Prince Didymos laughed and gestured for Kennet to go ahead. His good humor turned into complete horror as Kennet started checking every wall, every piece of furniture and every bit of fabric in the suite for hidden compartments, poisons or other threats. He sighed and settled on one of the chairs that Kennet indicated should be safe.

"This is going to be horrible," Prince Didymos sighed half an hour later as he studied the stack of things that Kennet deemed to be inappropriate for his presence.

"I did say that it would be, Your Highness," Kennet replied while tearing open one pillow to reveal a hidden packet of poison with a spring-loaded needle that could have killed Prince Didymos when he leaned against it. "I did say it would be."

Artifacts of Awareness is now available at all major retailers in ebook and TPB format.

OTHER BOOKS BY MEYARI
MCFARLAND:

Day Hunt on the Final Oblivion

Day of Joy

Immortal Sky

A New Path

Following the Trail

Crafting Home

Finding a Way

Go Between

Like Arrows of Fate

Out of Disaster

The Shores of Twilight Bay

Coming Together

Following the Beacon

The Solace of Her Clan

You can find these and many other books at www.MDR-Publishing.com. We are a small independent publisher focusing on LGBT content. Please sign up for our mailing list to get regular updates on the latest preorders and new releases and a free ebook!

AFTERWORD

Stubborn, scrappy characters are kind of my thing. My favorites are always the ones who won't ever give up, the ones who keep trying no matter what gets thrown their way.

Still, there's a point where keeping on isn't the right thing to do. Sometimes, walking away is the right choice. Sometimes, letting go is just what you have to do.

Ignatz couldn't do that so the apple tree did it for him.

I hope, if you're one of the stubborn ones like Ignatz and me, that you have someone to help you let go when it's time. And if you're the one dealing with a stubborn person refusing to give up on an impossible task, keep trying. You'll hopefully get through in time.

If you want more stories like this one, please go sign up for my newsletter on www.MDR-Publishing.com. You'll get updates on whatever I've got coming up, special deals and you can get a free ebook or collection of my short stories. Or you can sign up at my Patreon and get access to my art, writing and whatever's going on creatively in my life.

Thank you for reading!

Meyari McFarland
   March, 2024
   www.MDR-Publishing.com

AUTHOR BIO

Meyari McFarland has been telling stories since she was a small child. Her stories range from adventures appropriate to children to erotica but they always feature strong characters who do what they think is right no matter what gets in their way.

Meyari has been married for twenty years and has no children or pets. She lives in the Puget Sound, WA and enjoys the fog, rain and cool weather that are typical here. When vacation times come, she and her husband usually go somewhere warm like Hawaii or they go on their own adventures to Japan and other far away countries.

Her life has included jobs ranging from cleaning motel rooms, food service, receptionist, building and editing digital maps, auditing and document control.

MORE FROM MEYARI MCFARLAND

Website:

. . .

MEYARI MCFARLAND

www.MDR-Publishing.com

SOCIAL MEDIA:

Facebook - https://www.facebook.com/meyari.mcfarland.5
Pillowfort - https://www.pillowfort.social/Meyari
Pinterest - https://www.pinterest.com/meyarim/
Patreon - https://www.patreon.com/meyarimcfarland

If you enjoyed this story, please leave a comment on your favorite site. Also, please sign up for the newsletter so that you can hear about the latest preorders and new releases.

www.ingramcontent.com/pod-product-compliance
Lightning Source LLC
LaVergne TN
LVHW042003060526
838200LV00041B/1857